Love, Lucky

A Puppy of My Own

Wendy Loggia

A Skylark Book
New York · Toronto · London · Sydney · Auckland

RL 3.5, AGES 007–010

A PUPPY OF MY OWN

A Bantam Skylark Book / March 2001

ISBN: 0-553-48733-7

Visit us on the Web! www.randomhouse.com/kids

**Educators and librarians, for a variety of teaching tools, visit us at
www.randomhouse.com/teachers**

Published simultaneously in the United States and Canada

BANTAM SKYLARK is an imprint of Random House Children's Books, a
division of Random House, Inc. SKYLARK BOOK and colophon and BANTAM
BOOKS and colophon are registered trademarks of Random House, Inc.
Bantam Books, 1540 Broadway, New York, New York 10036.

For Olivia, with love.
Someday you'll have a puppy of your own. I promise.

Chapter One

"Fetch, Brighton!" Emily called, clapping her hands. "Come on, fetch!"

Brighton ran toward her, his fluffy tan paws flying over the grass and his pink tongue lolling out sideways.

"Get your stick, Brighton! Go!" Emily pointed behind him. Brighton skidded to a stop. Then he raced off in the direction he'd just come from.

Giggling, Emily pushed up her sleeve and checked her watch: 4:05. Eeks! How did it get so late so fast?

"Good boy, Brighton!" Emily said as the

Airedale terrier came bounding back, his long rubber stick in his mouth. She never let him play with wood sticks. He could easily get a splinter. "Time to go home," she told him.

Brighton dropped the stick at Emily's feet and looked up at her, his brown eyes hopeful.

His tail was hopeful too. Wag, wag, wag!

Emily reached into her jacket pocket. "See? I didn't forget." She rubbed the lint off a treat biscuit and handed it to Brighton. Just like always, Brighton gobbled it up.

Emily crouched down and clipped the leash onto Brighton's collar. If there was no one in the park, she let him run free, like today. But he had to wear his leash for the walk home.

"We had fun, didn't we, good boy?" she

said, rubbing one of his small doggie ears between her fingers. It felt like velvet.

They'd walked for twenty minutes. Then they'd stopped by the park and played all their old favorites. Fetch. Frisbee. Squirrel chasing.

Now, as they headed home, Emily patted Brighton's head and gave him another biscuit. The two of them turned down Ivy Street. There was hardly ever any traffic here, so Emily let Brighton run ahead of her. She held his leash.

Sometimes Emily had to put the brakes on—just to remind Brighton that she was in control. But that almost never happened. Except for the times they played fetch and Frisbee, Brighton was well behaved and usually liked to walk right beside her.

"Emily Conner!"

Emily turned around and squinted in

the late-afternoon light. Her two best friends, Kaia Hopkins and Lauren Parker, zoomed up on their bikes and came to a stop next to her.

Up ahead, Brighton barked. A happy bark. He was busy chasing a robin.

"Are you almost finished?" Kaia asked, slipping down off her seat so that her sparkle sneakers touched the pavement. Her long black curls bobbed up and down.

Emily loved Kaia's hair. Hers was straight. Boring. Nothing about Kaia was ever boring.

Lauren cupped her fingers tightly together and waved to Brighton. Her cheeks were almost as pink as her bike helmet. "Can you come ride bikes with us?" she asked breathlessly.

Emily shook her head. "I need to work on my family scrapbook before dinner." Just like last year, Emily, Kaia, and Lauren were in the same class at Curly Maple Elementary. Their third-grade teacher, Mrs. Williams, had said their scrapbooks weren't due until Monday. But Emily liked getting a head start on things.

"Are you sure?" Lauren asked, biting her lip. "Super-duper sure?" A leaf fluttered down and landed on one of her blond braids.

Emily nodded. Lauren always asked a lot of questions. "Maybe tomorrow."

Kaia pointed to the plastic bag Emily carried. "Ewww!" She wrinkled her nose. "I could never pick up dog poop."

Emily laughed. "I don't mind." Brighton bounded over to them and she scratched behind his tail. He liked that.

"Shhh, Kaia, you'll hurt his feelings," Lauren whispered.

"Do you think he understands me?" Kaia asked, peering into Brighton's dark eyes.

"Of course!" Emily said. "Dogs understand everything."

She and Brighton started walking. Kaia and Lauren trailed alongside.

"I can't wait until your birthday sleepover!" Lauren said, twirling the end of her braid while her other hand held her handlebars. Pink and green streamers dangled from them. "My mom said I can even drink soda." She lowered her voice. "That is, if you're having soda."

Lauren's mother was very particular about what Lauren ate.

Emily wasn't sure what they'd have to drink. She hadn't really thought much about it.

She was too busy thinking about her presents. About the one and only present she wanted for her birthday.

"Why, there's the splendid fellow now!" Mr. Virley was standing in his driveway waiting for them.

Brighton let out a bark and ran toward Mr. Virley.

He was Brighton's owner.

Emily ran too.

Mr. Virley was always calling Brighton "the splendid fellow." He had grown up in England. Emily, Kaia, and Lauren loved his accent. They all wondered if dogs in England had accents when they barked.

"How was your walk?" Mr. Virley asked, bending down to pat Brighton's back.

"Great," Emily said, handing over the leash and the poop bag. "We had so much fun in the park I forgot what time it was!"

Mr. Virley laughed and handed her four crisp one-dollar bills. "Thank you, Emily. You do a great job."

Emily loved walking Brighton. Mr. Virley had hired her as a dog walker at the beginning of the summer. He didn't like spending time outside—"Too blasted hot!"

he said. But he still wanted Brighton to get the exercise he needed.

Emily and Brighton had gotten along so well that Mr. Virley had asked if she'd like to keep dog walking once September came: twice a week, on Wednesdays and Saturdays. Her parents had said she could if she wanted.

And boy, did she want to! Because Emily loved dogs. Loved, loved, loved! She was even willing to walk Brighton for free.

But she didn't tell Mr. Virley that.

Emily carefully put the money in her zippered denim change purse, then patted Brighton on the head once more. "See you later," she said, blowing him a kiss. She waved to Kaia and Lauren as her two friends biked back down Ivy Street. Then, after checking both ways, Emily ran across to her lawn, her hair flying.

Her hands felt empty without the leash.

"But soon it will be my birthday," she whispered, skipping up the sidewalk.

And maybe she'd get the one and only present she wanted.

A puppy!

Chapter Two

"Organized and efficient," Emily said to herself later that afternoon as she kicked her legs back and forth under the kitchen table. That was what Mrs. Williams had said about Emily's classroom cubby. Emily had felt really good when she'd heard that.

She picked up a brown crayon and looked at her paper. *My Family,* she'd written carefully in green at the top. She'd already drawn her house with the red maple tree out front. Next came her mom and dad. Then Justin, her older brother. He'd taken the last poppy seed bagel this morning. So she'd given him beady eyes.

Emily drew Roadie, Justin's hamster, sitting on top of Justin's shoulder. Then she picked up a wheat-colored crayon. And she began to draw her puppy. A yellow Labrador retriever named Chippie.

Except she didn't have a yellow Lab named Chippie. She didn't even have any dog. But she wanted one so much!

Cocker spaniels. Boxers. Great Danes. Dogs, dogs, dogs! Everywhere Emily looked, she saw them. Trotting through her neighborhood. Barking on TV. Smiling doggie smiles in books and magazines.

Emily, Kaia, and Lauren *all* wanted dogs.

"We're too busy for a dog!" Kaia's mom said.

"Well . . . I'll think about it," Lauren's mom said.

"No," Emily's mom said.

So there they were.

Emily's situation was the worst. Worst, worst, worst! Because Kaia already owned two pets. She had Gertie the goldfish. And whiskery Purr was her cat.

So Kaia wasn't as desperate as Emily was.

Lauren didn't have any pets. But Emily knew her friend always got what she wanted. Pretty soon—*poof!*—she'd get one. Only, Lauren had a hard time making choices. It would probably take her a little while.

Emily didn't have that problem. She knew everything there was to know about yellow Labrador retrievers.

How big they grew. (Big!)

The food they ate. (Lots and lots of dry stuff!)

The toys they liked. (Squeakies and chewies!)

Where they liked to be. (In the water, just like Emily on a hot summer day!)

And most important of all, yellow Labs were smart, friendly, and loving!

A yellow Lab. That was her dream. A puppy—that she could cuddle and teach and play and grow up with!

Just as Emily was putting the finishing touches on Chippie's ears, Justin came running in. As usual, he tracked mud all over the kitchen floor.

"Justin." Mom looked up from where she stood rinsing tomatoes at the sink and frowned. "Did you remember to wipe your feet?"

"Sorry," Justin said, dashing back to the doormat.

"And did you bring the garbage can back to the house?" she continued. Emily and Justin both had after-school chores. Emily always did hers first thing when she got home.

Justin didn't.

Her brother groaned and ran outside, letting the door slam.

Mom sighed.

Emily went back to her drawing. She just needed to get the little part where the ear flopped over. . . .

The door slammed again. "Done!" announced Justin. He ran over and gave Emily a noogie.

"Hey!" she cried, glaring at him.

"Feet, Justin," Mom reminded.

He looked down at Emily's drawing. " 'My family'?" he read, pointing to the words and then to the picture. "Double duh, Emily. We don't have a dog!" he said, laughing.

Emily felt stung. *Duh yourself, Justin,* she thought angrily as Justin tore upstairs to his room.

Of course she knew they didn't have a

dog. "I was drawing Brighton!" she yelled out.

But as she stared down at her paper, the smooth yellow hair, the soft rounded ears, the thick tail, and the big black eyes that gazed back at her looked nothing like Brighton, the Airedale terrier.

They looked like her Chippie. The yellow Lab.

I gave young Emily a lovely workout at the park today. She threw that red plastic saucer to me at least ten times. Then she still wanted to carry on! So we moved to the stick. Humans worry me, though. Truly, they do. To think that some of them wonder if we dogs understand them! My oh my. And they have the most peculiar behaviors. Take young Emily, for example. After all this time, you would think the little lass would learn to hold fast. But no. Each and every time we go to the park, she loses that stick—just like Master Virley! In fact, she loses it many, many more times than he does! Then it's up to me to go and find it. Perhaps someday I'll be able to train her properly.

Brighton

Chapter Three

"More bread?" Mom asked, holding up the basket.

Emily nodded, reaching for a slice. She could eat garlic bread every night.

"Mrs. Manning gives us so much homework," Justin complained, stabbing his spaghetti. "I spend all afternoon doing it."

"Life's rough," Dad said with a wink. He poured some salad dressing on his lettuce. "Anything special happen today, Em?"

"I walked Brighton," she answered. "He was so much fun!"

"Did he roll over and play dead?"

Justin asked. He leaned back in his chair, closed his eyes, and held up his hands as if they were paws.

Emily rolled her eyes. "Very funny."

"Justin," Mom said. "No dogs at the table."

"Having a real dog wouldn't be any different from having Justin around," Emily said, making a face at him.

"Here we go again." Justin groaned.

Emily shot him a look before turning to her parents. "Can't I get a puppy? Please?" Emily and her parents had had this conversation before. Actually, they'd had it lots of times. Emily hadn't managed to persuade them to change their minds.

But there's always a first time, she told herself.

"Puppies turn into dogs," Dad said. He always said that.

"I know, Dad. But I could take care of a

dog," she began. "And I've done lots of reading," she went on. "Ask me anything."

"Who is the president of France?" Justin asked.

"About dogs," Emily said, exasperated.

Mom laughed.

Emily took that as a good sign. "I'm very responsible. Just ask Mr. Virley. He'll vow for me."

"I think you mean 'vouch,'" Dad said, wiping his mouth with his napkin. He and Mom exchanged glances.

"I haven't let Brighton down once," Emily said, looking from one to the other.

"You've really been a help to Mr. Virley," Mom said. "I'm proud of you."

Emily beamed. Things were going her way! And she'd been saving the best for last. "I've gotten an A-plus on every spelling quiz, I always do my homework, and I never need to be reminded to make my bed or set the table." *Like some people,* she thought, sneaking a peek at Justin. He was too busy eating to notice.

Emily held her breath. Usually this was where it happened. This was when her parents shot her down. She knew the list of reasons by heart.

1. Dogs are expensive.
2. They need company.
3. They need someone to feed and brush them—not just play with them when you feel like it.
4. Dogs need exercise.
5. Dogs need to be trained.
6. If you go away, you need to find a place for your dog to stay.

But tonight her parents didn't say any of the usual things. Instead, they just kept eating. "May I be excused for a second?" Emily asked. Before Mom could answer, Emily ran over to her book bag and pulled out some library books she'd borrowed for extra ammunition. "See?" she said, running back to the table. "I'm learning everything about yellow Labs."

"Well, Emily, you've given us a good list of reasons about why you should get a dog," Dad said, tossing his napkin aside.

"It *is* my birthday on Friday," Emily reminded him, just in case they'd forgotten.

"We know, honey. I just bought everything for your party today," Mom said. Then she stood up and began clearing the table. "Whose turn is it to dry?"

Emily chewed her lip. It wouldn't do any good to keep begging. She could tell Mom didn't want to talk about it anymore.

But for once, her parents didn't come out and say no. They didn't say yes . . . but they didn't say no, either.

And there *were* those weird looks they kept giving each other. And hadn't Emily heard them whispering when she walked into the kitchen before dinner?

Emily hopped up and grabbed a dish-towel. Maybe they'd planned everything already.

Maybe she was going to get a puppy after all!

Chapter Four

Emily sat up straight in her seat as Mrs. Williams passed out some sheets of paper Thursday morning. It was language arts time, and Mrs. Williams was talking about the main idea of a story. She had a fuzzy cow pin fastened to her pale blue shirt.

Emily loved language arts. Reading was one of her favorite things.

Justin, on the other hand, was not one of her favorite things, she thought, scowling. Today had started out bad and it was all his fault. First her pesky brother ate all the toasted oats. She had to have bran flakes for breakfast. Yuck. Then he made her laugh when she brushed her teeth and she dribbled toothpaste on her shirt. Double yuck. But the worst was when he forgot his math homework and Mom had to drive all the way back home just so he could get it.

That made them late.

That meant she'd missed morning lineup outside.

That meant she hadn't been able to talk to her friends yet.

Just then Zoe Cho, in the seat beside her, tapped her shoulder. "Psst!" she whispered, dropping something into Emily's hand. It was a note. *Big News!* was written in purple ink on the outside.

Emily made sure Mrs. Williams wasn't looking. She put the note in her lap and carefully unfolded it.

Dear Emily,

Where were you? I have BIG NEWS.
Reelly, reelly, BIG NEWS! I'll tell you and
Kaia (who was late too—like always) at
lunch.

Luv U Forever,
Lauren

P.S. Want to trade cookies?
P.P.S. I have choklit chip!

Emily glanced at her teacher. She
didn't want to get in trouble for passing
notes. When Mrs. Williams got angry, she
got real, real quiet. That was even scarier
than yelling.

Mrs. Williams handed out some sheets
of paper. "Now we're going to talk about
fantasy and reality," she said. "If something is real, it could happen. If something is fantasy, it couldn't happen."

Emily peeked over at Lauren. "I can't
wait!" she mouthed.

Lauren's dimples dimpled.

What could it be? Emily tried to run through the possibilities in her mind, but there wasn't time. She had work to do!

She looked down at the paper on her desk. There were eight sentences on it.

"I want you to write 'Real' or 'Fantasy' next to each sentence," Mrs. Williams told the class. She wrote *Real* and *Fantasy* on the board. "Then I want you to write your own Real sentence and your own Fantasy sentence."

This was going to be fun! Emily read the first sentence. *Fish can fly.* She giggled. *Fantasy*, she printed carefully next to it. Then she read the second sentence. *I can find a good book at the library. Real,* she wrote.

She worked her way down the list. Now she had to make up her own sentences. Easy! *Justin will never bug me again,* she wrote for her Fantasy sentence.

Now the next one. *I'm getting a dog!* she wrote for her Real sentence, using the I'm Someone Special! pencil Mrs. Williams had given out the first day of school.

Beside her, Zoe's stomach growled. "I'm hungry!" Zoe whispered, making a silly face.

"Me too," Emily whispered back, stealing a look at the clock. Hungry for Lauren's big news!

"You'll never believe it," Lauren said as she, Emily, and Kaia waited in the milk line at lunch. She looked from Emily to Kaia and back to Emily again.

"Try me!" Kaia said, jiggling her change. Her hair was pulled up in two ponytails, each with a strawberry-shaped ponytail holder.

"Yes, tell us!" Emily begged. She could hardly wait.

Lauren picked up a carton of milk. "Promise you won't get mad?" she asked them. Her forehead crinkled.

Emily was puzzled. "Why would we get mad?"

"Well . . ." Lauren paused. "I'm getting a puppy!"

"You are?" Kaia burst out.

"That's great!" Emily exclaimed. Now she'd have someone to go dog walking with!

"Superbly great!" Kaia said. "Why did you think we would be mad?"

Lauren waited while Emily handed her quarters to the cafeteria lady. "I know you both want dogs. I didn't want to hurt your feelings."

They trooped over to the section where the third-graders sat. The lunchroom wasn't a cafeteria at all—it was the Curly Maple auditorium. The janitors set up tables for lunch. Unless there was an assembly.

Emily dove into her seat. "Tell us about your puppy, Lauren!"

"What kind are you getting?" Kaia asked, sliding in beside her.

Lauren sat down and rested her chin in her hands. "We can't decide! I want one that's cute and fluffy. Like my cousin Joey's Westie. My mom wants one that's small and doesn't shed."

"How about a poodle?" Kaia asked, opening her milk.

Lauren shook her blond head. "Not enough fluff."

Emily opened her milk, then reached in her red lunch bag cooler and pulled out a ham and cheese sandwich. She hadn't planned on telling her friends about her birthday present. But now, with Lauren's big news, she couldn't keep her secret any longer!

"Guess what?" she told her friends. "I'm getting a puppy, too. Tomorrow!"

"You are?" Kaia's wide brown eyes went wider.

"What kind?" Lauren asked, bouncing in her seat.

Emily sucked in her cheeks and crossed her fingers. "I think—*I think* it will be a yellow Lab."

"Just what you want!" Lauren exclaimed.

"Luckies," Kaia mumbled. She took out a chicken sandwich and a container of baby carrots from her purple vinyl lunch sack.

Emily and Lauren looked guiltily at each other. "Uh-oh," Emily whispered, knowing how sad Kaia probably felt. No one liked to feel left out.

"Don't feel bad, Kaia," Lauren said, patting her shoulder. "You can be our puppies' aunt. We can take them to the park together." Lauren held her peanut butter sandwich tight. "Maybe they'll even become best friends like us!"

Kaia smiled.

"Yeah!" Emily said happily. She licked some mustard from her lip. "Yellow Labs are the best," she declared. "Just ask the Earl of Malmesbury."

"Huh?" Lauren said.

"Who?" Kaia asked.

Emily giggled. "The Earl of Malmesbury. He had a lot of yellow Labs and he used their skills in the water on his estate. It was somewhere in England. I bet Mr. Virley has heard of the earl."

"Boy, you know a lot about dogs," Lauren said admiringly.

"About yellow Labs," Emily corrected. "I have to if I want to be a responsible dog owner."

"How did you find out you're getting a puppy?" Kaia asked.

Emily checked to make sure Justin wasn't anywhere near them. "We talked about it at dinner last night. My parents didn't say for sure, but they're getting me one for my birthday. I just know."

Kaia suddenly looked doubtful. "Are you positive?"

"Maybe you just think you are," Lauren said, scrunching her mouth. "Maybe your parents are getting you a movie *about* puppies."

Emily knew that wasn't true. "No, they know that's all I want." She thought of how responsible she'd been these past few months. And how well she'd presented her case. And how Mom and Dad had looked at each other when they didn't think she was watching.

She gave a firm nod. "It's a done deal."

"You're really lucky," Kaia repeated with a sigh. "With Kristy and Bug and Gertie and Purr, I don't think I'll ever get a dog. There're too many Hopkinses already." Kristy was Kaia's older sister. She was a fourth-grader at Curly Maple. Bug was her younger sister. She was four.

"You never know," Emily said, sucking up the last few drops of milk with her straw.

"Do you think you'll have the puppy at your party?" Lauren asked.

"Maybe," Emily said slowly. "Maybe I will!" One thing was for certain, she thought as she crushed her milk carton. With a yellow Labrador there, her sleepover was going to be more like a no-sleepover!

Chapter Five

Sunlight streamed through Emily's bedroom blinds onto her carpet. She kept her eyes closed for a moment. Then she popped them open. Everything in her room looked the same—but she was different. She was eight!

This was the day she'd been waiting for forever. Fingers, toes, and eyes crossed, it was the day she'd finally, finally get her puppy!

"Tomorrow I won't need the sunshine or Mom to wake me up," she told the ceramic yellow Labrador statue on her

shelf. "I'll have wet kisses on my nose instead!"

Hopping out of bed, she went to the
bathroom, then rushed back to her room
and put on her new white knit shirt and
embroidered jeans, a gift from her aunt
Sophie. Mom had let her open the pack-
age last night.

"Mmm mm mm mm mm mmhhh,"
she hummed as she brushed her static-y
shoulder-length dark brown hair, study-
ing her reflection in the mirror. Was it her
imagination, or did she suddenly look
more mature? Same hair, same brown
eyes, same tiny gap between her front
teeth. Still, there was something. . . .

Emily studied the gap. Pretty soon her
front left tooth would fall out. She'd use
her tooth fairy money to buy a present for
Chippie!

"Well, if it isn't the birthday girl," Mom
said as Emily skipped into the kitchen.

Mom leaned over and kissed Emily on the cheek. "Happy birthday, honey."

Emily slipped into her usual chair. "Thanks, Mom."

Mom slid a plate in front of her.

"Chocolate chip pancakes!" Emily cried. "Cool! It isn't even the weekend!"

Mom grinned. "Look what else." She took a can of whipped cream from behind her back and gave it to Emily. "Go for it."

"Yay!" Emily began drawing smiley whipped cream faces on her pancakes.

"What's this I hear about someone having a birthday?" Emily's dad said as he walked into the kitchen. He pretended to be confused. "Is it someone in this house?" He lifted a leaf on Mom's plant. "Is it you, Mr. Fern?"

Emily groaned. "Dad."

He bent down and kissed her head. "Happy birthday, Em." Then he swiped a finger through a whipped cream smile and popped it in his mouth. "Yum!"

Justin stumbled into the kitchen, still in his pajamas. "You guys are so loud."

"I'm only two years younger than you now," Emily singsonged, cutting her pancakes. The whipped cream had melted into little rivers. But it still tasted delicious.

Justin's eyes widened. "Chocolate chip pancakes?"

Mom nodded. "You'd better hurry if you want some. The bus leaves in fifteen minutes."

"The bus" was the Conner minivan.

"You have to be nice to me today," Emily warned Justin as he drank his juice.

He shrugged. "Okay. You can have the bathroom first."

Emily sat back, pleased. She'd already

used the bathroom, but she'd take small victories where she could get them.

"Em, there's a surprise in your lunch-box," Dad said as he lifted his car keys from their hook. "But no peeking."

Emily's heart skipped a beat. Would it be a note telling her she was getting her dog?

"And tonight's the big night," Mom said, smiling. "I can't wait to see all your friends."

Four-legged friends, you mean! Emily thought excitedly as she stuffed the last piece of pancake into her mouth.

The best day of her life had finally arrived!

" 'Happy birthday to you,' " Emily's class-mates finished singing.

Emily smiled at her friends. Whenever it was someone's birthday, Mrs. Williams had everyone sing. And then the birthday person got to pass out whatever special treat they had brought in.

Emily had pink-frosted cupcakes and grape juice boxes.

"I hate pink," said Andrew Crane, sticking out his tongue.

"Then don't eat it," Emily said, doing her best imitation of her mother. She handed one to Kaia.

"Thanks, Emily," Kaia said, making a face at Andrew.

Andrew scowled. But he unwrapped his cupcake anyway.

When Emily returned to her seat, everyone was allowed to eat. And when they were finished, Mrs. Williams said it was time to work on today's spelling words.

Pencil. Pillow. Dolphin. Emily copied down the words Mrs. Williams wrote on the board, but it was hard to concentrate.

In between each word, she drew a little dog bone.

When Emily had finished her list, she looked up at the clock. The big hand was on the six. The little hand was on the ten.

They were in the middle of spelling. Still to come were social studies and lunch and reading and math. Emily guessed there were about four hours left until school let out.

Four hours until she'd meet Chippie!

Chapter Six

What: Emily's 8th Birthday Sleepover!
When: Friday, September 21st
Where: 124 Ivy Street
Time: 7:00 p.m.
For: Emily Joy Conner
Please bring: Your pj's, a sleeping bag, & a photo of you and your favorite animal!

"**P**erfect, perfect, perfect!" Emily danced across the family room. They'd pushed the furniture to the corners, leaving a nice big open space for sleeping bags. Mom had hung streamers around the windows, and had arranged bowls of tortilla chips and M&M's on the coffee table.

"Honey, before your friends come we want to give you your presents," Mom said.

"Hooray!" Emily shouted. This was the moment she'd been waiting for all day. All month! All year! All her life!

Excited, she sat down on the plump stuffed chair, which was now pressed against the wall. Mom went out and came back in, her arms piled high. Emily's dad and Justin were behind her. Dad had the camera. Justin had a box wrapped in comics.

"Happy birthday, sweet pea," Mom said, dropping the presents on the ottoman and giving Emily a big hug.

Emily hadn't expected so many presents. Taking a deep breath, she ripped open the first one. "Cool! A Jenny doll!" she exclaimed, holding her up. Justin rolled his eyes.

"You can borrow her if you want," she told him, giggling. Mom laughed too.

The next present was *Little Paws*, one of Emily's all-time favorite movies. She even had a poster of Scribbles, the cute Tibetan terrier movie star, hanging in her room. "You girls can watch it tonight," Mom suggested.

"Thanks!" Emily said, giving *her* a hug. Next she opened the latest two *Sweet Treat Club* books. Then came a pretty bracelet made of pink stones. She tried it on and Dad took a picture. And then a board game. And a blue sweater and matching skirt.

With each gift, Emily grew more excited.

"Oooh, how sweet," she said when she opened Justin's present. For once he hadn't gotten her something he wanted himself. Inside the box was a fuzzy brown dog with a small pink tongue! Underneath it was a silver yo-yo with lightning bolts.

"Here, let me show you how to do it," Justin said quickly, picking up the yo-yo and unhooking the string.

"Well, at least half the gift is for me," she joked as she gave the stuffed dog a squeeze.

Then she looked around. That was the last present in sight. "Is that all?" she asked, anxious. "Didn't you get me something else?"

Mom and Dad looked at each other. "There are a lot of nice things, here, Em," Dad said.

Emily waved her hand in the air. "I know . . . but . . ." Her voice drifted off.

"Some gifts you have to wait a little longer for," Mom said, gathering up the torn wrapping paper. "Just be patient."

"That's right," Dad said. He reached

over and messed up her hair. "Better get moving now."

Emily sat there for a moment, clutching the dog. Dad popped some M&M's in his mouth and turned to Justin. "What do you say we men go bowling?"

Justin slapped Dad five. "Anything to get me away from Giggleville."

"Get your jacket and I'll meet you in two and two," Dad said. "Have fun, Em," he told Emily, kissing the top of her head.

Emily could barely give him a wave.

A sinking feeling came over her.

Emily looked up at Mom. A lump formed in her eight-year-old throat. "I've been patient," she said in a small voice.

Mom didn't hear her. "Aren't you excited about seeing your friends?" she asked, stooping to grab a bright blue bow. "This is your biggest sleepover ever."

Her friends? Emily didn't know how

she could face them. She'd told everyone she was getting a dog. Disappointment washed over her like cold gravy.

"I don't want a party anymore," she said, sticking out her lower lip. "Call everyone up and tell them I changed my mind."

Mom bent down and looked Emily in the eye. "Now, why would you want me to do that, Emily?" She reached over and smoothed back Emily's hair.

Emily stared over at her birthday presents. Tears filled her eyes. "Because I've been patient all year! The one thing I wanted for my birthday I didn't get," she cried. She kicked the video across the carpet. "I wanted a dog. A real dog!" Sobbing, she threw Justin's present on the floor and stomped on it. Dumb stuffed dog.

Mom stood up. "In this house, when we get presents, we don't throw them or kick them," she said calmly. "I'm very sorry you're disappointed, Emily. But your friends will be here in thirty minutes. And they are expecting a party."

Mom picked up the video and put it on top of the TV. Then she walked out of the room.

Emily sniffled. She pouted. But pouting by herself didn't do much good. It didn't do much good to pout in front of her parents, either. She'd learned from experience that they didn't like pouters.

Emily knew she had acted like a baby. But she didn't care. *After all, I'm not nine or anything,* she thought, hiccuping. She was eight.

Eight years old.

This morning, she had thought eight had sounded very grown-up. But now she wasn't so sure.

When would she be old enough to have a puppy of her own?

Chapter Seven

"I love eating pizza like this," Lauren confided, letting the cheese dribble into her mouth. "Don't you?" She sat cross-legged on her sleeping bag, a napkin across her lavender-nightgown-covered lap.

"Hm-mmm," Emily told her, propping herself up on her elbows.

"I'm not even homesick," Lauren added with a whisper. "Sometimes that happens when I spend the night at someone's house."

"You can always call your mom if you want," Emily told her. "My mom said."

Lauren smiled gratefully. "Once I get my dog, I won't leave him for a second." The minute she'd arrived, Lauren had told Emily they'd decided to get a bichon frise. "Don't you think bichons are the cutest?" she asked now.

Emily was about to answer when a piece of popcorn dinged her on the head.

"Score!" yelled Kaia, waving her arms in the air. The other girls giggled.

"Do it again," Emily asked, sitting up. This time Kaia aimed for her mouth. Emily scooted forward and caught it with one bite. Everyone applauded.

Emily wished she could have invited everyone she liked at Curly Maple to her sleepover. But the Conner rule was you could have as many guests as you were years old.

There were Jessica and Maddie from her soccer league. Annie, Zoe, and Brittany from her class. And her friend Sarah

Maxwell from tap. Emily didn't tap anymore. But she still was friends with Sarah. And of course Lauren and Kaia were there.

All the girls were in pj's. And they were all sprawled out on the family room floor, chowing down and watching *Little Paws*.

Emily had managed to stop crying before her friends arrived. She had washed her face and blown her nose. And when Kaia and Lauren asked about Chippie, she just shook her head. Luckily, they were good friends. They didn't ask her any more questions.

She did have fun when she opened her presents. Then they ate ice cream cake *first,* before Emily's mom brought in the platter of hot nachos and the delivery guy came with two steaming pizzas. The pizza place had made an "8" in pepperoni. Everyone thought that was really cool.

When Emily had blown out her candles after the birthday song, she had still wished for a puppy. But she knew it wasn't looking good.

When it had been time to do the craft she and Mom had decided would be neat—a Popsicle-stick picture frame with a picture of each girl and her favorite pet or animal—Emily had felt like crumbling. She used a picture of herself with Old Rosie, a horse she'd ridden at the New York State Fair.

If it's not Chippie, who cares who's in the picture? she'd thought glumly, squeezing glue on a Popsicle stick.

"Whoever falls asleep first gets potato chips in their sleeping bag," Jessica announced now, braiding Sarah's long black hair.

Kaia giggled. "And cheese puffs in her ears. But we're not going to sleep until midnight!"

"And we'll paint her fingernails blue

and green," Maddie announced, holding up two of the tiny bottles Emily had received as a gift.

"Won't we get in trouble?" Lauren asked, worried.

"Shhh, you guys!" Zoe pointed to the TV, then held a finger to her lips.

Annie's round face was anxious. "This is the good part."

Everyone quieted down.

Lauren snuggled beside Emily, crunching a chip. Emily loved this movie. But seeing Scribbles tear down the street following a trail of dog bones only made her feel worse. A tear slid down her cheek as she stuffed herself deeper in her sleeping bag, hoping no one had seen.

Eight-year-olds didn't cry.

Unless they really, really felt like it.

Chapter Eight

"More pancakes, Brittany?" Mom asked, waving her spatula.

Brittany yawned. "No thank you, Mrs. Conner."

"Sounded like you girls had fun last night," Mom said, pouring the rest of the pancake batter on the sizzling griddle. "You were still going strong at midnight!"

Emily rubbed her eyes. She was pooped. After *Little Paws* had ended, they had played a card game. After that, everyone decided Jessica had done such a good job braiding Sarah's hair, she should do everyone else's. Then Mom had made another huge bowl of popcorn, and they made lists of their favorite things and took turns guessing whose was whose. When Zoe fell asleep first, everyone had taken turns decorating her.

That was before Maddie got mad at Jessica and Annie got mad at Kaia. But then everyone made up, so it was okay.

Emily had crashed facedown in her sleeping bag sometime after two. She'd still be sleeping if Justin hadn't stood in the doorway this morning and rung his dumb cowbell, waking them all up.

Now the girls were wolfing down a special pancake and bacon breakfast. Emily knew her mom wasn't happy with her. Her smile didn't have the sparkle it normally did.

Emily did feel kind of bad for still being mad at her mom and dad.

But they had disappointed her badly. *So they deserve to be disappointed by me,* she thought, staring at her orange juice.

"Ooh, your mom's here, Annie," Kaia said, looking out the window. Annie hopped off her stool and grabbed her overnight duffel from the floor.

"Thanks, Emily. I had a lot of fun." She turned to Emily's mom. "Thank you, Mrs. Conner."

"Don't forget your goodie bag," Emily reminded, handing her friend one of the blue cellophane treat bags she and her mom had made. Inside were sidewalk chalk, a pack of licorice, a Crazy Eights card game, and a sticker sheet of Dalmatians.

Pretty soon all the other parents came. Then it was just Lauren and Kaia. Their moms said they could stay a bit later.

"Want to come walk Brighton with me?" Emily asked her friends.

Lauren clapped her hands. "Can I hold the leash part of the way?"

"Sure," Emily said.

Kaia stretched. "Don't you feel like skipping today? I'm so tired."

"I can't skip," Emily explained. "Mr. Virley is counting on me." She opened up a cabinet and found the box of biscuit treats her mom had bought for when she walked Brighton. She stuffed a few in her pocket.

"Bye, Mom," she said, opening the door. Normally she kissed Mom good-bye. But not today. Today all she did was wave.

Emily and her friends walked over to Mr. Virley's house and went around to the gated backyard. As usual, Brighton was waiting.

"Ruff! Ruff, ruff!" he barked. Those were his guard dog barks. Then he recognized Emily.

His tail wagged. "Ruff! Ruff, ruff!" Those were his love barks!

Emily unlocked the gate and expertly clipped the leash onto the Airedale's collar.

"Hi, Brighton!" Lauren said, giggling as he licked her face. "We're going to take you for a walk."

Kaia patted his black and tan coat. "Hi, cutie." She and Lauren walked out to the driveway. Emily followed, shutting the gate behind them. The four of them started down Ivy Street.

Emily's heart felt heavy. She had to talk to her friends. "So I didn't get a puppy," she said softly.

Kaia walked in between her and Lauren. "You must be sad."

"I am," Emily admitted.

"Then we're sad too," Lauren said firmly. "I bet even Brighton would be sad if he knew you were."

"Dogs know when their owners are sad," Emily told them. She'd read that in a library book.

Brighton stopped to bark at a butterfly. After he showed it who was boss, he started trotting once more.

"I don't know what to do," Emily said, dejected. She swung the leash back and forth. "I'm all out of ideas."

"Volunteer at an animal shelter," Kaia suggested. "My aunt does that. You'd be around animals all the time."

Emily wasn't quite sure what a volunteer did. But being around dogs all day sounded like fun. "Maybe," she said slowly. "But I still want a puppy of my own."

"You could check out all the Web sites about dogs," Lauren said. "That's what my dad's been doing. That's where we read about bichons." She skipped along. " 'Friendly, fluffy, and fun.' That's what bichons are."

"Where will you get a bichon?" Kaia wanted to know.

"A friend of my mommy's," Lauren explained as they turned the corner onto Holly Avenue. "She has a bunch of puppies that all need homes. Isn't that lucky?"

It sure was. Emily handed Lauren Brighton's leash. "Here, Lauren. You'd better practice."

Chapter Nine

"How about this one?" Lauren asked, holding up a wide brown leather collar for Emily to inspect.

Emily shook her head. "That's for a bigger dog. You want something smaller." She pointed to a display of dainty jeweled collars. "Like those."

"Oooh," Lauren said, lifting a white one off the metal bar. "This is pretty." She turned to her mom. "Can we get this one, Mommy?"

"I don't see why not." Mrs. Parker tucked a long strand of blond hair behind her ear and smiled at Emily. "You've been a great help today, Emily honey. I'm glad you could join us." That afternoon, Emily's parents had had some errands to run. Justin was at his friend Tyler's house playing video games. And Emily was spending the afternoon with Lauren.

Emily had wanted to have a tea party with Lauren's pretty pink china tea set. "Or we could try out the paper-doll-making software I got for my birthday," she'd suggested when Mom had dropped her off at the Parkers' house.

Lauren had stopped her. "I've got an even better idea," she'd said excitedly. "My mom said she'd take us to Pet Parade! Won't that be fun? You can help me pick out everything for our bichon frise."

The idea of going to Pet Parade had made Emily want to cry. But she didn't have the heart to say no.

Now Emily shrugged sheepishly. "I just

want you to get the right things." She'd helped Lauren and her mom choose a nice, soft beanbag doggie bed. And a gold metal identification tag so they could put their address and phone number on it in case their dog got lost. And a soft-bristle brush for combing their bichon's coarse and curly white hair.

Pet Parade was a really great store. They had everything you could imagine. Emily loved their TV commercials, and their slogan, "For the Dog Who *Thinks* He Has It All!" But Pet Parade wasn't just for dogs.

It was for the birds, too!

And cats, hamsters, and even tropical fish and reptiles. When you walked out of Pet Parade you realized that there were a lot of pets to choose from!

Emily sighed. She was a one-pet girl. Only a dog would do. And while it was fun helping Lauren, it also made her sad. As Mrs. Parker stopped to look at some food bowls, Emily couldn't help feeling that *she* should be the one shopping for a dog.

"Those kind are good," Emily said, pointing to some medium-sized metal bowls. She picked one up and turned it over. "See? It's heavy, so the dog can't carry it around. She won't be able to knock it over, either."

"That's a nifty idea," Mrs. Parker said, putting one in their shopping cart. She even picked out a weighted water bowl to match.

"Our dog is going to be so happy," Lauren declared as her mom picked up a bag of gourmet dog food.

"She sure will," Emily agreed, feeling glum again. She was trying hard to be excited for Lauren. But the truth was, she was jealous. Emily hopped on one foot. Jealous. She hopped on the other foot. Jealous. She jumped on both feet.

Why can't my mom know anyone with a dog? she thought enviously. Why did Lauren always get everything she wanted?

Lauren always had new shoes. Expensive new shoes. And new shirts. New jeans. And her bedroom was filled with fun toys and dolls. Every time Emily went over to Lauren's house, there was always something new to play with.

Suddenly Emily realized that Lauren's dog was going to be just like Lauren! She already had a shopping cart full of new things. Not only that, but Mrs. Parker said that once they got their dog, they'd probably have to come back and pick up all the things they forgot!

Emily was sure they didn't forget anything. Collars. Leashes. Food bowls. Beds. Emily noticed that Lauren's mom didn't check the prices at all. Anything Lauren wanted just—*pop!*—went into the shopping cart.

Emily's mom didn't shop that way. Emily bet that Mrs. Parker never cut coupons. Emily bet Mrs. Parker never told Lauren to wait until Christmas.

Without meaning to, Emily began to sulk.

A few seconds later, Lauren's eyes filled with concern. She slapped her hand over her mouth. "Oh, Emily," she said. "Am I being a bad friend? Am I making you feel bad about not getting a dog for your birthday?"

"No!" Emily burst out quickly. "I'm fine."

"Are you sure?" Lauren asked doubtfully. "You look kind of sad again."

Emily nodded, forcing herself to smile the way she did on picture day. "I'm sure," she lied.

Lauren kicked at a piece of paper on the floor. "I wish you could have a dog, too, Emily," she said softly.

Emily hunched her shoulders. "So do I."

"You can pretend my dog is yours," Lauren said. "You can walk her and play with her whenever you want. Just like Kaia will."

Emily appreciated her offer. But it just wouldn't be the same. She pointed to where Mrs. Parker had stopped up ahead. "Look! Doggie sweaters!" Anything to stop Lauren from feeling sorry for her.

The girls ran over. "Isn't this adorable?" Mrs. Parker asked, holding up a fleecy red dog coat. "It even has matching boots!"

Lauren and her mom tried to decide what color to buy.

Now Emily was really blue. Not only wasn't she getting a dog—she missed her mom. Her coupon-cutting, loving mom.

She and her mom had fun together. Always. Now Emily couldn't help remembering her mom's face when she'd dropped Emily off at Lauren's house. Emily had jumped out of the car without even a hug. Mom had looked very sad.

Now Emily was the one who was sad. Trying not to cry, Emily turned her eyes to a poster tacked to the wall above her. *Are You a Responsible Pet Owner?* she read. A list of things that responsible pet owners did was below.

There were lots of questions that Emily couldn't answer. For example, *Do you give your dog enough exercise?* Or *Does your dog always have fresh water?* But at the bottom of the poster, there was a picture of a smiling boy standing beside a beagle. Next to the pair were the words *Be kind and generous to your pet. Your pet will thank you . . . with his love.*

Emily thought of how she walked Brighton each week. Even if it rained. Even if she was exhausted. Yes, she decided, she was responsible.

Then Emily thought of how she and Mom baked fudge brownies once a month for the church soup kitchen. And the time she had loaned Ben Brooks her favorite green pencil with the purple fuzzball on the tip. She'd had to use her boring yellow pencil all day. That was kind.

Or what about when she let Zoe sleep with Fairy Rabbit the night of her slumber party because Zoe had forgotten her teddy bear? Wasn't that generous?

Yes, Emily realized. *Yes, it was! I* am *a kind and generous person.* But knowing this didn't make her happy. Instead, she felt terrible! Because a generous friend would be happy for Lauren.

So what if Lauren had everything? She

was nice. She was sweet. *She is a great friend,* Emily thought suddenly.

"Emily, I'm going to take Lauren to the bathroom," Mrs. Parker called over.

"Do you need to go?" Lauren whispered loudly.

"No."

"You need to come with us, anyway," Mrs. Parker said. But when Lauren and her mom went inside the ladies' room, Emily snuck to the front of the store.

She had only a few minutes. She'd have to act fast.

They had passed a big pen of squeaky toys when they'd arrived. Emily hurried there now. She pulled a bright orange toy in the shape of a bone from the pile. Then she ran to the cash registers and opened her change purse.

"That will be four dollars, please," the woman told her.

Good! Emily knew how to count four dollars. She offered the bills Mr. Virley had given her that morning. The woman handed her a plastic Pet Parade bag with the toy inside.

A toy Emily was positive Lauren's new bichon frise would love.

Just a Li'l Pawprint from Me

Yip! Guess what? I heard my human mama on the telephone. I'm going to get a new mama named Lauren! Yip! Yippee! Yip! I hope her hands are warm and gentle. I have a feeling we're going to be the best of friends.

My Rules for Lauren

Toys! Give me toys!
Chew sticks!
A beanbag bed. No old blankets!
No other dogs allowed near my house.
(This means the lawn, too!)
Lots of brushing.
Not much bathing.
Those warm fuzzy things that keep you warm.
A nice name.

I might sound picky. But I'm a bichon frise.
I'm allowed to be!

Chapter Ten

My bedroom ceiling has a crack in it, Emily thought, resting her head in her pillows and staring up. *A long, thin, ugly crack.* She frowned. What did that matter? She couldn't very well put *that* in her family scrapbook. *Emily Conner's ceiling has a crack.* Working on her scrapbook was what she was supposed to be doing, instead of lying here daydreaming.

But Emily was scrapbooked out. She'd done all the drawings and filled out what information she could. It was just that there were some questions she couldn't answer. *What was your mother's life like when she was your age? Your grandmother's?*

Emily sighed. She would have to ask Mom.

But she couldn't ask Mom without talking to Mom.

And she hadn't spoken to Mom all day. She hadn't even told her about the stuff Lauren had picked out at Pet Parade.

It wasn't that she didn't want to talk to her. It was that she didn't know how. She was embarrassed. She knew she'd been wrong. But it was hard to say she was sorry.

Every time Mom had tried to talk to *her*, Emily had pretended not to listen. Even though she had wanted to. She just couldn't make herself do it.

She'd sat in church quietly. She'd put on her play clothes quietly. She'd eaten her Sunday lunch of pot roast and mashed potatoes quietly. Now she was working quietly.

Mom had sat quietly beside her. Then

she had sighed and got up. "I'll be down-stairs if you want to talk, honey. Love you." Emily had listened to Mom's feet as they went downstairs.

Emily was alone. And it was really quiet.

The worst quiet of all.

She took a big, brave breath. "Mom?" she said in a soft voice.

Quiet.

"Mom?" she called, a bit more loudly.

More quiet.

Then, "Mom?" she yelled. She'd had a lot of practice using that voice.

"Yes?" came Mom's voice up to Emily's bedroom.

Emily swallowed. "Can you help me, please?"

The sound of Mom's feet padded up the stairs. Mom stuck her head in Emily's doorway. "Sure, honey. What's up?"

Emily pointed to her family scrapbook,

which lay next to her on her quilted bed-spread. "I can't do this."

Mom came in and sat down next to Emily. Emily showed her the questions. Mom nibbled on a fingernail. "Hmmm. What was life like when I was young?" She pretended to frown. "You mean I'm not still young?"

Emily let out a giggle. "Um, no."

"Oh. Okay then." Mom drummed her fingers on the paper. "Let's see. When I was your age . . . well, there was no Internet. No VCRs or video stores. No CDs. And no fried mozzarella sticks."

Emily's jaw dropped. "No fried mozzarella sticks?" They were her favorite!

Mom shook her head. "I had a bereft, deprived childhood, Emily."

"Huh?" Emily asked.

Mom laughed. "Lots of things were different. But lots of things were the same, too. I had my own favorite series of books to read, just like you do. And I liked to play Parcheesi, just like you. My favorite color was blue, just like yours is. And"—Mom paused—"I loved dogs. Especially yellow Labs. Just like you."

Emily's eyes widened. "You did?"

Mom nodded. "But Grandma and Grandpa wouldn't let me get a dog. Uncle Tim is allergic to animal hair—just seeing it makes him sneeze. So I couldn't have any pets with fur." She grinned. "I had to settle for a fat goldfish named Meyer."

Poor Mom! "But then you have to know how much a dog means to me," Emily said, although she couldn't imagine anyone, even her own mother, wanting a dog as much as she did.

"I think I do," Mom said quietly. She pointed back to the scrapbook.

"Lauren's getting a bichon frise," Emily said.

"Heather told me," Mom said. Heather was Mrs. Parker. "I bet Lauren's excited."

"She is," Emily said. She thought of being at Pet Parade and how she had missed her mom yesterday.

Emily looked down at her hands. "I'm sorry I yelled at you on my birthday," she told her. "I'm sorry I threw the video. And Justin's toy."

"Me too," Mom said, wrapping her arm around Emily's shoulders and pulling her close. "I don't like to see you get upset. Especially on a special day."

Emily snuggled against her mom, the familiar smell of soap and vanilla perfume comforting her. "I just felt so sad. All I wanted was a puppy."

Mom kissed the top of her head. "Well, Dad and I have a surprise that we think will make you happy."

Emily's heart leapt.

"We've been planning on taking you and Justin there tomorrow. Somewhere special."

Emily's heart slumped down. She sank against Mom. "Oh. Okay." Mom was being so nice that Emily couldn't act ungrateful again. If Mom and Dad were taking her and Justin somewhere for a treat, it could only mean two things:

a. She wasn't getting a dog.
b. She was going to Pizza Partee.

Not that Emily had anything against Pizza Partee. In fact, it was one of her most favorite places to eat ever. But you had to be in the right mood to enjoy all the lights and games and Justin running around screaming. Emily just wasn't in that kind of mood at all.

Without a dog, the wind had gone out of her sails.

And the bark had gone out of her bite.

Chapter Eleven

"Hi, guys. How was school?" Dad asked when Emily and Justin climbed into the minivan.

"Okay," Justin said, fastening his seat belt.

"Ditto," Emily said, fastening hers. Normally Mom came alone to pick them up. But today Dad had left his office early to join them. She couldn't believe he was willing to go to Pizza Partee. He always got a headache when they ate there.

Emily wasn't even that hungry. She

sank back in her seat as they pulled away from Curly Maple Elementary.

"I scored two runs in kickball," Justin said. He pretended to kick an imaginary ball with his foot.

"That's great!" Mom said, turning around in her seat to smile at him.

"A butterfly got in our room today," Emily said, trying to think of something just as exciting to tell her parents. "He had orange wings. Mrs. Williams opened a window and he flew out."

"That's nothing," Justin told her. "Once a blue jay was trapped in the library. He sat right on top of the display case. Mr. Fripp chased him for twenty minutes."

Emily stuck her tongue out at her brother when her parents weren't looking. Then she looked out the window. Buildings. Trees. Kids on bikes. Kids who didn't have scratchy seat belts digging into their skin.

They drove.

And drove.

And drove.

Sunshine shone through the moon roof. Emily was hot. And getting pretty darn tired of riding. They'd been driving for hours. Days. *Years.*

Emily watched out the window as they whizzed past a vegetable stand. Why was her dad going on the back roads? Pizza Partee was right next to the mall.

"This isn't the way to Pizza Partee," she whispered to Justin as they drove by an old farm silo.

His mouth opened. "We're going to Pizza Partee?" he exclaimed. "Cool!"

Emily scratched her head. "Well, I *thought* we were. But look out there. This is the wrong way. And you know, it is kind of early for dinner."

She stretched forward. "Dad! Where are we going?" she asked.

He reached back and gave her shoe a tug.

"Just a few more minutes and you'll see," Mom said over her shoulder.

Emily poked Justin in the arm. "Where did you think we were going?"

Justin rolled his eyes. "If you don't know, I'm not telling."

Emily made a face. "You don't know either, dorkhead." She said it low, though. Mom got mad if they called each other names.

Wide-open farmland flew by Emily's window. Now Emily wasn't bored. Now she was trying to solve a mystery.

Where were they going?

Exactly fifteen minutes later, Dad pulled up to a large white house with a big front porch and a dirt driveway.

"We're here!" he said, turning off the ignition. A wooden sign hung from a post. Plum Valley K. C., it said.

"Where's here?" Emily asked her mom.

Mom's eyes were twinkling. "You'll see."

Everyone got out of the car. Emily could tell Justin was just as confused—and curious—as she was.

"Go on back," Mom said, pointing to the rear yard.

Emily and Justin raced each other to the fence. Justin unlocked the gate.

The first thing Emily saw was a tall red-haired woman wearing jeans and a green T-shirt standing next to a huge fenced-in pen.

The first thing she heard were barks. Puppy barks!

The woman turned to wave. "Hi there! You must be Emily and Justin. I'm Angie. Come on back."

Emily ran over and peered in the pen. Inside were a grown yellow Labrador . . . and six puppies! "Mom! Mom, come quick!" Emily shouted. She had never

seen anything so cute in all her life. The puppies were running and jumping. Tumbling and bouncing. Rolling. Sniffing. And squiggling and wiggling.

"Can I pet one?" Emily asked Angie. Little goose bumps danced up and down her arms. She'd never seen a yellow Lab puppy in person. They never looked this soft and cuddly in her books!

Angie bent down and lifted up a squirming ball of fur.

"How about this one?" she said, gently handing the puppy to Emily. "It's a she."

Emily giggled as the puppy licked her face and arms and neck. "Her tongue feels like sandpaper!" she squealed, loving every wet second.

"Better get used to it," her dad said from behind her. Emily blinked. Her heart pounded. Her hands sweat. The goose bumps tripled.

"This little wiggleworm belongs to you," her mom said tenderly, patting the puppy on the head. "Happy birthday, honey."

Emily gazed down into the puppy's soft biscuit-colored face. A little rough tongue tickled her nose. Silky stiff whiskers tickled her cheeks. "She's mine?" Emily gulped. "For real?"

"We wanted to have her for your birthday, but she wasn't quite old enough to leave her mama," her dad said, putting his arm around her. "Mom and I made several trips out here while you guys were at your friends' houses or at school. This puppy is the one we liked best."

Emily couldn't speak.

"We wanted to tell you on Friday. Remember I said to be patient?" Her mom tilted her head. "You weren't in a listening mood."

For a moment Emily felt small. Criminal. Terrible. Her mom and dad had planned to get her a puppy all along! If only she *had* been more patient, the fight would never have happened.

The puppy nibbled her ear. "Hey!" she squealed, squeezing the puppy tight.

The puppy?

Her puppy!

The sad moment passed. Emily would never be sad again. How could she? She had a puppy! "Thank you," she cried, hugging her parents and the puppy all at once.

The puppy yelped. Emily pulled back. "Sorry!"

Everyone laughed.

"Are we taking them all home?" Justin asked, reaching into the pen and petting some of the other pups.

Angie laughed. "Nope, just her. The others all have families waiting for them."

"Puppies need to be eight weeks old be-fore they can leave their mom," Emily said.

Angie nodded. "At least. That's how old your puppy is."

Suddenly Emily's eyes filled with warm tears. She'd wished for this day to happen, and now, here it was! She buried her face in the puppy's fur so Justin couldn't see her. Boy, would he make fun.

But wait! Emily glanced up. That sound . . . Emily knew that sound: a cross between a hiccup and a wheeze.

"You're crying too!" Emily exclaimed, looking at her brother. She giggled through her tears.

"Am not!" Justin said, scowling. He dragged his sleeve across his face. "Is she just Emily's dog?" he asked their parents.

"She's Emily's special birthday gift,"

Mom said, ruffling his hair. "But she'll belong to all of us. Right, Em?"

Emily nodded, peppering the puppy's silky head with kisses. Who had time to talk?

She was too busy falling in love!

Woof! Lick! Woof!

Woof! Where am I? I'm in a box! Woof! The world is a lot bigger than I thought. So is this house! There's lots to chew on here!

Sob! Woof! Sob! Woof!

I miss Mama! And my brothers! And my sisters! Mama told me I'd have my own human someday.

I guess I didn't think it would happen so soon.

But boy, that little girl is nice. She told me her name is Emily. And she talked to me the whole way here. I was scared, too.

We were in a car. And we were moving! I didn't like that very much.

We stopped at the vet's. I didn't like that very much either. I was ready to leave right away! Sob! Woof! Maybe I can fall asleep here. It is awfully warm and soft. Emily kissed my nose! And she gave me food and water. She gave me a soft blankie and a bottle that felt really warm. "To help you sleep," she said. She told me she was going to sleep in her room, but that she would play with me all day tomorrow. Whenever that is! You know what? Emily is the nicest person I ever met! I'm going to give her a big wet kiss as soon as I see her. Woof!

Chapter Twelve

"**S**o after we left the breeder's, we took the puppy to the veterinarian for a health check," Emily explained during lunch the next day. She popped a cheese puff into her mouth. She had taken only three bites of her sandwich. She'd been too busy talking.

"Did he give her shots?" Lauren asked, covering her eyes.

"Yes, but it was quick," Emily told Lauren's fingers. The puppy had let out a small squeak. That was all.

"Then what did the vet say?" Kaia asked.

"That she's perfect!" Emily said happily. "The breeder gave us a list of things we need to know, and a feeding chart so we'll feed her the right food at the right times."

"I bet you knew it all already," Kaia said, looping her fingers under her jumper straps.

"Not everything," Emily admitted. "This is the first time my puppy's been away from her litter. I didn't think about her being scared."

The puppy had cried for a long time last night. Dad had gotten a hot water bottle from the closet and Emily put it in the crate. That had helped.

"When can we see her?" Lauren asked.

"As soon as you want," Emily said eagerly. She couldn't wait for her friends to see how cute her puppy was!

"Guys, I have an idea!" Lauren leaned forward. Her purple-ribboned braids swished along the table. "Let's start a club! A dog club!"

Emily and Kaia looked at each other, their eyes wide.

"I'm getting a bichon frise, Emily's got her puppy, and Kaia's mom is thinking about letting her have a dog," Lauren went on. "It's perfect!"

"Count me in!" Emily cried.

"My mom will have to let me get a dog if I'm in a dog club," Kaia said excitedly.

Lauren grabbed each of their hands. "We'll have club rules and everything!"

"Dog walking!"

"Pet sitting!"

"Pet kissing!"

"Puppy parties!"

"And secret pawshakes!" Kaia finished, her arms outstretched.

"Should we start our club now or wait until we all have our dogs?" Lauren wondered, nibbling a pretzel stick.

"Maybe we can start planning the club now but not really *be* a club until you both get dogs," Emily proposed.

"Okeydokey," Lauren said. "I'll start thinking of clubby stuff."

Kaia smiled. "Bring your puppy over to my house, Emily! Once my parents see how lovable she is, they'll want one too!"

Everyone munched lunch.

"You guys can borrow my dog books if you want," Emily told her friends a minute later. "I just need to look through them one more time. I need to find a name."

All along, Emily had dreamed of having a dog named Chippie. But somehow her yellow Lab puppy didn't look like a Chippie. She looked like . . . she looked like . . . Emily was stumped.

Kaia blew her milk straw wrapper across the table. "You still don't have a name picked out?"

Emily blew the wrapper back. "Nope."

"How about Princess?" Lauren suggested.

Emily thought that would be better for a tiny dog. But she didn't want to hurt Lauren's feelings. "She doesn't look like a Princess," she said diplomatically.

"What about naming her after a place you've been to?" Kaia asked.

Emily had been to New Jersey, Florida, Pennsylvania, and Ohio. "Um, I don't think so," she said.

"How about after her color, like Goldie?" Lauren asked.

That wasn't a bad idea, but . . .

Talking about naming the puppy made Emily start to *think* about her puppy. And thinking about the puppy made her *miss* the puppy.

She couldn't wait to get home!

"What am I going to name you, furball?" Emily said, holding the puppy over her face. Emily lay on her back on the kitchen floor. The dog's little legs wriggled back and forth and her tummy was soft and downy and round.

Mom had taken very good care of the puppy while Emily was at school. She'd fed her and given her plenty of water. Mom had even cut up an old, soft blanket in squares for the puppy to play with.

"You better watch out or she'll go wee-wee on you," Justin said, crunching into a granola bar. "Puppies do that."

Emily wrinkled her nose. "My puppy won't. I'm lucky."

A bell went off in her head. "Lucky! That's it!" she yelled. That was the perfect name for her dog! Because Emily was lucky. Lucky to have such nice parents, lucky to have an okay brother, lucky to have such good friends, and lucky to have found a perfect dog like . . . Lucky!

Not Chippie or Princess or Florida. Lucky!

"Do you like Lucky for a name?" she asked Justin eagerly.

Justin swallowed his granola. "That works. You're in luck, squirt."

Mom and Dad liked Lucky too.

So Lucky it was!

That night, when it was time for bed, Emily crouched down and gazed at Lucky's furry face. The puppy was curled up in her bed inside her crate. Her eyes were heavy.

"I love you, Lucky," Emily whispered, sticking her fingers in through the bars and stroking the soft, wrinkly fur above Lucky's eyes, and then her velvet paws.

Lucky was fast asleep. Her little chest moved up and down. Little breaths of air sighed from her mouth.

Lucky slept a lot. But Emily knew that would change, and that her puppy would grow into a dog she would keep loving for years and years and years.

"I love you, Lucky," Emily whispered once more. Lucky. The perfect name for the perfect puppy.

The perfect birthday present.

DOG TIPS

HOW TO PICK
THE RIGHT DOG FOR YOU!

Choosing the right dog for your family is no easy task. There's a lot to consider. Do you live in an apartment or do you have a house with a large yard? Is someone home to walk your dog during the day or will your dog be alone? How much time do you think you can spend grooming: brushing, bathing, and doing regular doggie up-keep things, like trimming nails? Who will train your dog?

There's a lot to think about . . . but the effort will be worth it! Here are some tips that can help you make the best choice.

🐾 Is everyone in your family willing to pitch in and help with your new dog? Sometimes you might forget to feed your dog. Or you might not feel like walking him or cleaning up his messes. But just like people, dogs need to be fed on a regular schedule and to have the right amount of exercise. Having everybody in your family ready to feed, walk, groom, and discipline your dog will make owning a pet a much happier experience for everyone!

🐾 Owning a dog isn't cheap. You'll need to buy dog food every week. Leashes, collars, and trips to the vet all cost money. Sometimes other expenses come up too, like paying for a dog trainer, or a kennel if you want to go on vacation and can't take your dog along. And what if your dog chews up your furniture . . . or your favorite shirt? These things all have to be considered before you get a dog.

🐾 How old are your siblings? If you have a brother or sister who is under three, think carefully about getting a dog. Little kids can sometimes be rough with pets, so you may need to look for a dog that doesn't mind some horseplay. Although each individual is different, certain breeds—like golden retrievers and beagles—are known to be excellent with children. The sex of a dog might be something to consider too. While dogs of both sexes make great pets, sometimes females are calmer.

🐾 Responsibility! If you've ever asked for a dog, you've probably heard this word. And for good reason! A lot of responsibility comes with having any pet—but especially a dog. You'll need to take him to the vet if he's sick—and to make sure he has his shots. Feed him and give him fresh water every day. Take him for walks. Keep him free of fleas by using flea collars and baths. Wash dirty dog dishes. Clean up if he poops on your rug. And give him lots of love.

Some things to look for when you choose a puppy:

- A strong body
- A wet—not runny—nose
- White teeth—and fresh breath!
- Clean eyes, free of any gunk or goop
- Clean ears
- Soft, flea-free fur
- Sturdy legs
- A clean bottom

Although you can't always avoid problems, this checklist can start you thinking about what you need to know.

How to Choose a Breed

Where do you live? If you live in a tiny apartment, an Irish setter may not be the best choice. But if you live where she could get plenty of exercise, that might be the dog for you. Not all owners of large dogs have large spaces for them to run in. But as anyone who owns a Saint Bernard can tell you, a big fenced-in yard can be a good thing! The climate plays a part too. If you live somewhere that's really hot—or really cold—you may need to take that into consideration.

☙ Does dog hair bother you or your parents? Some dogs shed a lot, while others, like bichons frises, don't. But bichons need to be clipped and groomed regularly—another expense. Shih Tzus and Old English sheepdogs are really cute—but keeping them brushed and looking good takes a lot of hard work. Decide how much time—as well as how much money—you can spend.

☙ Not all dogs come from breeders. Adopting a dog from an animal shelter or rescue organization is a wonderful option. Every city has shelters occupied by dogs of all shapes, ages, sizes, and breeds that are looking for good families to love them. Sometimes these dogs have been mistreated by their former owners. They may have special needs. Or maybe they were given up because their former owners couldn't care for them properly. The people who work at the shelter can help you make a good choice for your situation. You can also ask a local veterinarian for more advice. Giving a shelter dog a home can be a great way to find your dog!

🐾 Your family's lifestyle and expectations are super-important when making your decision. Make sure you know the reason why you want a pooch to join your family. Is it to play with you? Maybe a mixed breed is the way to go. To keep you company when you're lonely? Try a loyal cavalier King Charles spaniel. Bullmastiffs are ideal guard dogs. Maybe an older dog is more suited to your family.

Don't assume that small dogs are easy to take care of and big dogs are difficult. That's often not the case!

A dog really can be your best friend. So make sure to choose one that you can love for his whole lifetime. If you know why you truly want a dog, the experience will be better for everybody—including your dog!

Your parents will count on you to take good care of your dog . . . and your dog will be counting on you too!

About the Author

Although she does not presently have a dog, Wendy Loggia has always loved them. Growing up, she was the proud owner of Rebel, a Siberian husky–German shepherd mix; Muffins, a toy poodle; and Nuisance, an adorable mutt who was part of her family for fifteen years. She's looking forward to the day when a furry-legged friend curls up at her feet again!

Make Your Dog Famous!

Win a chance for your dog to be included in an upcoming Woof! book.

Think your dog is the cutest canine ever?
Then enter your mutt's mug in our contest and, if you win, your dog's picture will appear in an upcoming Woof! book! Second and Third prizes are also available. To enter, write a paragraph explaining why *your* dog is the picture-perfect pooch! Attach a photo of your dog and send it to:

Picture-Perfect Pooch Contest
Random House Marketing Dept.
1540 Broadway, 19th Floor,
New York, NY 10036.

See **official contest rules** on the next page or visit our Web site at **www.randomhouse.com/kids**

Official Rules & Regulations

I. HOW TO ENTER

NO PURCHASE NECESSARY. Enter by printing your name, your parent's name, your dog's name, your address and phone number, your date of birth, and a paragraph (250 words or less) stating why your dog is the picture-perfect pooch on a 3" x 5" index card. Attach a photo of your dog and mail to: Picture-Perfect Pooch Contest, Random House Marketing Department, 19th Floor, New York, NY 10036. Contest ends May 30, 2001, and all entries must be received no later than 5:00 p.m. Eastern Time on that date. LIMIT ONE ENTRY PER PERSON. Entries (including photographs) will not be returned.

II. ELIGIBILITY

Contest is open to residents of the United States, excluding Puerto Rico and the state of Florida, who are between the ages of 7 and 10 as of May 30, 2001. All federal, state, and local regulations apply. Void wherever prohibited or restricted by law. Employees of Random House, Inc., its parents, subsidiaries, and affiliates, their immediate family members, and persons living in their household are not eligible to enter this contest. Random House, Inc., is not responsible for postage due, lost, stolen, illegible, incomplete, or misdirected entries.

III. PRIZES

Grand Prize

One winner will have his/her dog's likeness, name, or photo appear in an upcoming Woof! book to be determined by Random House Children's Books.

Second Prize

Ten runner-ups will each receive a Picture-Perfect Pooch dog tag for their dog's collar.

Third Prize

One-hundred entries will receive a Picture-Perfect Pooch paper picture frame.

Approximate retail value of total prizes is $500 U.S.

IV. WINNER

Winners will be chosen on or about June 15, 2001, from all eligible entries received within the entry deadline by the Random House Marketing Department. Entries will be judged by Random House Marketing Department staff on the basis of originality, style, and creativity; decisions of the judges are final. The prize will be awarded in the name of the winner's parent or legal guardian. Random House will not be able to return your entry; please keep a copy for your records. Winners will be notified by mail on or about June 30, 2001; no other entrants will be notified. Taxes, if any, are the winner's sole responsibility. RANDOM HOUSE RESERVES THE RIGHT TO SUBSTITUTE PRIZES OF EQUAL VALUE IF PRIZES, AS STATED ABOVE, BECOME UNAVAILABLE. Winner's parent or legal guardian will be required to execute and return, within 14 days of notification, affidavits of eligibility and release. A noncompliance within that time period or the return of any notification as undeliverable will result in disqualification and the selection of an alternate winner. In the event of any other noncompliance with rules and conditions, prize may be awarded to an alternate winner.

V. RESERVATIONS

Entering the contest constitutes consent to the use of each winner's name, likeness, and biographical data (and the use of the name and likeness of each winner's pooch) for publicity and promotional purposes on behalf of Random House with no additional compensation or further permission (except where prohibited by law). Other entry names will NOT be used for subsequent mail solicitation. For the names of the winners, available after June 30, 2001, please send a stamped, self-addressed envelope to: Random House, Picture-Perfect Pooch Winners, 1540 Broadway, 19th Floor, New York, NY 10036.